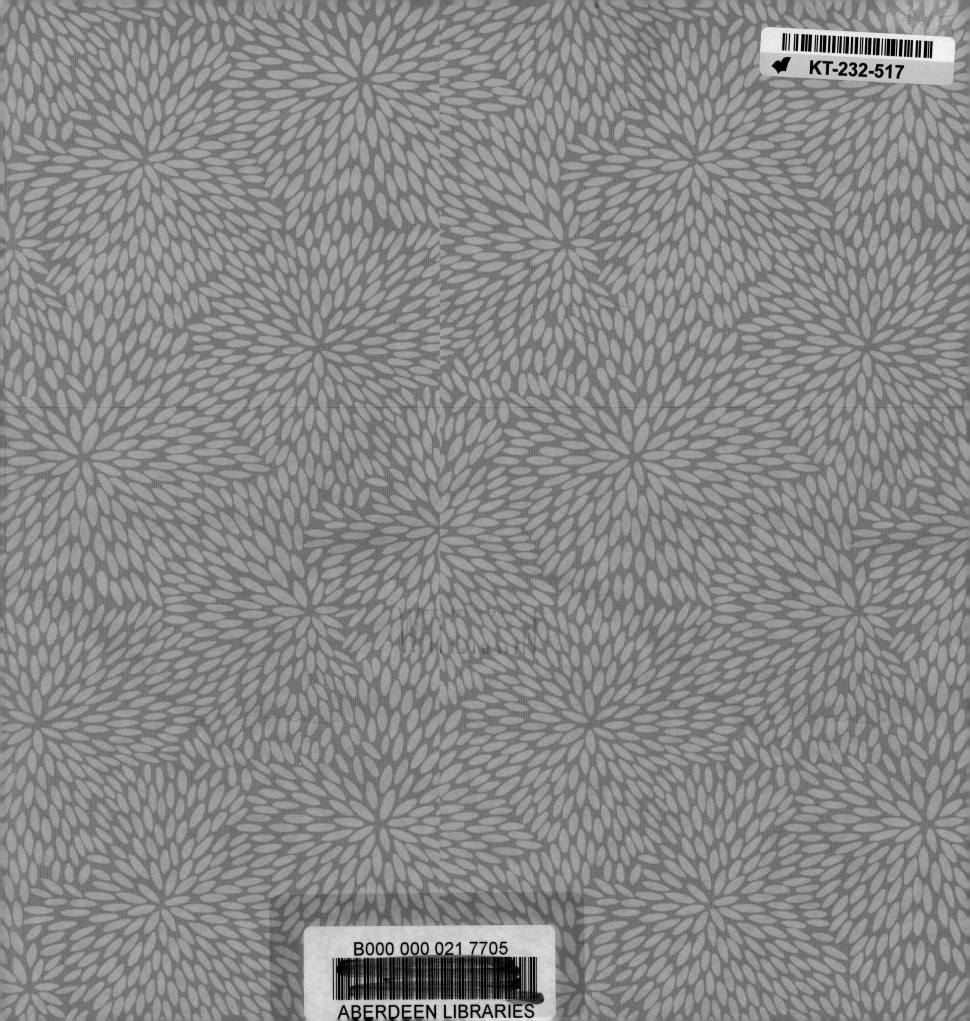

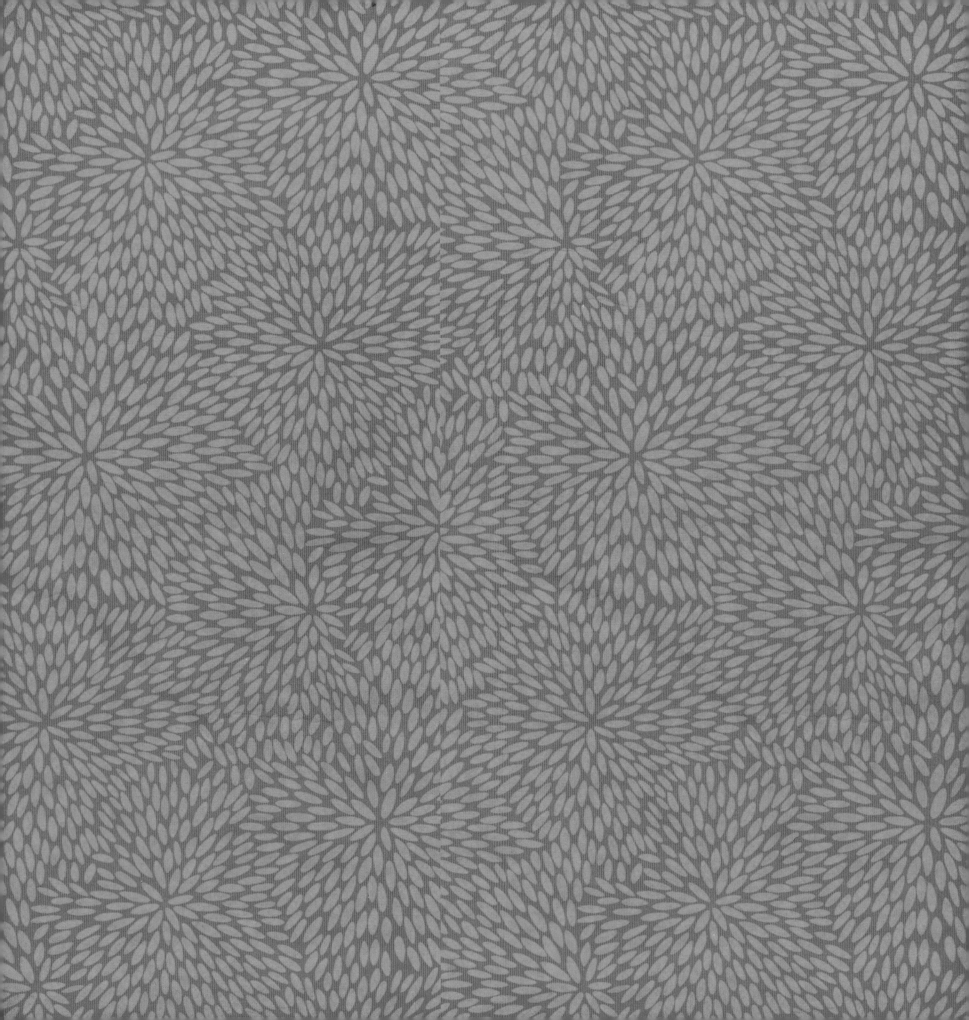

I See the Moon

Rosalind Beardshaw

nosy crow

Golden Slumbers

Golden slumbers kiss your eyes,
Smiles awake you when you rise.
Sleep, pretty baby, do not cry,
And I will sing a lullaby.

Cares you know not, therefore sleep,
While over you a watch I'll keep.
Sleep, pretty baby, do not cry,
And I will sing a lullaby.

Twinkle, Twinkle, Little Star

Twinkle, twinkle, little star,
How I wonder what you are!
Up above the world so high,
Like a diamond in the sky.

When the blazing sun is gone,
When he nothing shines upon,
Then you show your little light,
Twinkle, twinkle, all the night.

Then the traveller in the dark
Thanks you for your tiny spark.
How could he see where to go,
If you did not twinkle so?

In the dark blue sky you keep,
Often through my curtains peep,
For you never shut your eye,
Till the sun is in the sky.

As your bright and tiny spark
Lights the traveller in the dark,
Though I know not what you are,
Twinkle, twinkle, little star.

Star Light, Star Bright

Star light, star bright,
First star I see tonight,
I wish I may, I wish I might,
Have the wish
I wish tonight.

Flying

I saw the moon,
One windy night,
Flying so fast –
All silvery white –
Over the sky
Like a toy balloon
Loose from its string –
A runaway moon.
The frosty stars
Went racing past,
Chasing her on
Ever so fast.
Then everyone said,
"It's the clouds that fly,
And the stars and moon
Stand still in the sky."
But I don't mind –
I saw the moon
Sailing away
Like a toy
Balloon.

J. M. Westrup

Bedtime

The evening is coming,
The sun sinks to rest.
The rooks are all flying
Straight home to the nest.
"Caw!" says the rook as he flies overhead.
"It's time little people were going to bed!"

The flowers are closing,
The daisy's asleep.
The primrose is buried
In slumber so deep.
Shut up for the night is the pimpernel red.
It's time little people were going to bed!

The butterfly, drowsy,
Has folded its wing.
The bees are returning,
No more the birds sing.
Their labour is over, their nestlings are fed.
It's time little people were going to bed!

Thomas Hood

Girls and Boys Come Out to Play

Girls and boys come out to play,
The moon is shining bright as day.
Leave your supper and leave your sleep,
And come with your playfellows into the street.
Come with a whoop and come with a call.
Come with a good will or not at all.

Wee Willie Winkie

Wee Willie Winkie runs through the town,
Upstairs and downstairs in his nightgown,
Tapping at the window, crying through the lock,
"Are the children in their beds?
For now it's eight o'clock!"

Bed in Summer

In winter I get up at night
And dress by yellow candlelight.
In summer, quite the other way,
I have to go to bed by day.

I have to go to bed and see
The birds still hopping on the tree,
Or hear the grown-up people's feet
Still going past me in the street.

And does it not seem hard to you,
When all the sky is clear and blue,
And I should like so much to play,
To have to go to bed by day?

Robert Louis Stevenson

Hush-a-Bye, Baby

Hush-a-bye, baby,
On the treetop,
When the wind blows,
The cradle will rock.
When the bough breaks,
The cradle will fall,
And down will come baby,
Cradle and all.

Sleep, Baby, Sleep

Sleep, baby, sleep,
Your father tends the sheep,
Your mother shakes the dreamland tree
And from it fall sweet dreams for thee,
Sleep, baby, sleep.

Come to the Window

Come to the window,
My baby, with me,
And look at the stars
That shine on the sea!
There are two little stars
That play at bo-peep
With two little fishes
Far down in the deep,
And two little frogs
Cry, "Neap, neap, neap.
I see a dear baby
That should be asleep!"

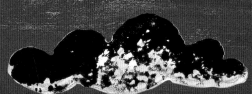

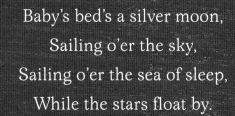

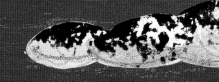

Baby's Bed's a Silver Moon

Baby's bed's a silver moon,
Sailing o'er the sky,
Sailing o'er the sea of sleep,
While the stars float by.

Sail, baby, sail
Far across the sea,
Only don't forget to come
Back again to me.

Baby's fishing for a dream,
Fishing near and far,
Her line a silver moonbeam is,
Her bait a silver star.

Sail, baby, sail
Far across the sea,
Only don't forget to come
Back again to me.

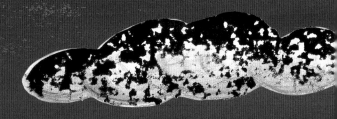

Hush, Little Baby

Hush, little baby, don't say a word,
Papa's going to buy you a mockingbird.

If that mockingbird won't sing,
Papa's going to buy you a diamond ring.

If that diamond ring turns to brass,
Papa's going to buy you a looking glass.

If that looking glass gets broke,
Papa's going to buy you a billy goat.

If that billy goat runs away,
Papa's going to buy you another today.

Good Night, Sleep Tight

Good night, sleep tight,
Don't let the bedbugs bite.
Wake up bright
In the morning light
To do what's right
With all your might.

The Man in the Moon

The man in the moon
Looked out of the moon
And this is what he said,
"It's time that, now I'm getting up,
All babies went to bed."

I See the Moon

I see the moon,
And the moon sees me,
Shining through the leaves of the old oak tree.
Oh, let the light that shines on me
Shine on the one I love.

To Amber,

with love, Ros x

First published 2017 by Nosy Crow Ltd
The Crow's Nest, Baden Place, Crosby Row
London SE1 1YW
www.nosycrow.com

ISBN 978 1 78800 082 6

Nosy Crow and associated logos are trademarks
and/or registered trademarks of Nosy Crow Ltd

Collection © Nosy Crow 2017
Illustrations © Rosalind Beardshaw 2017

The right of Rosalind Beardshaw to be identified as the illustrator
of this work has been asserted.

A CIP catalogue record for this book is available from the British Library.

Printed in China

Papers used by Nosy Crow are made from wood grown in
sustainable forests.

1 3 5 7 9 8 6 4 2

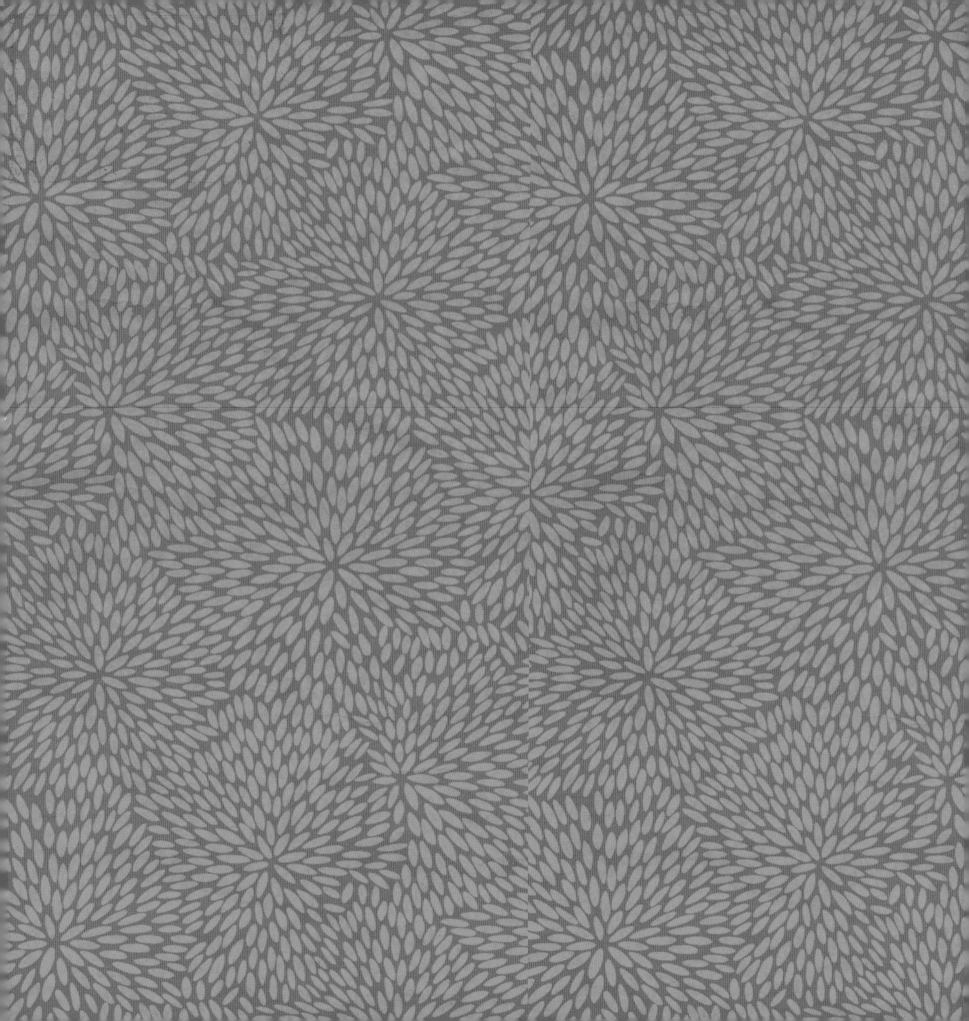

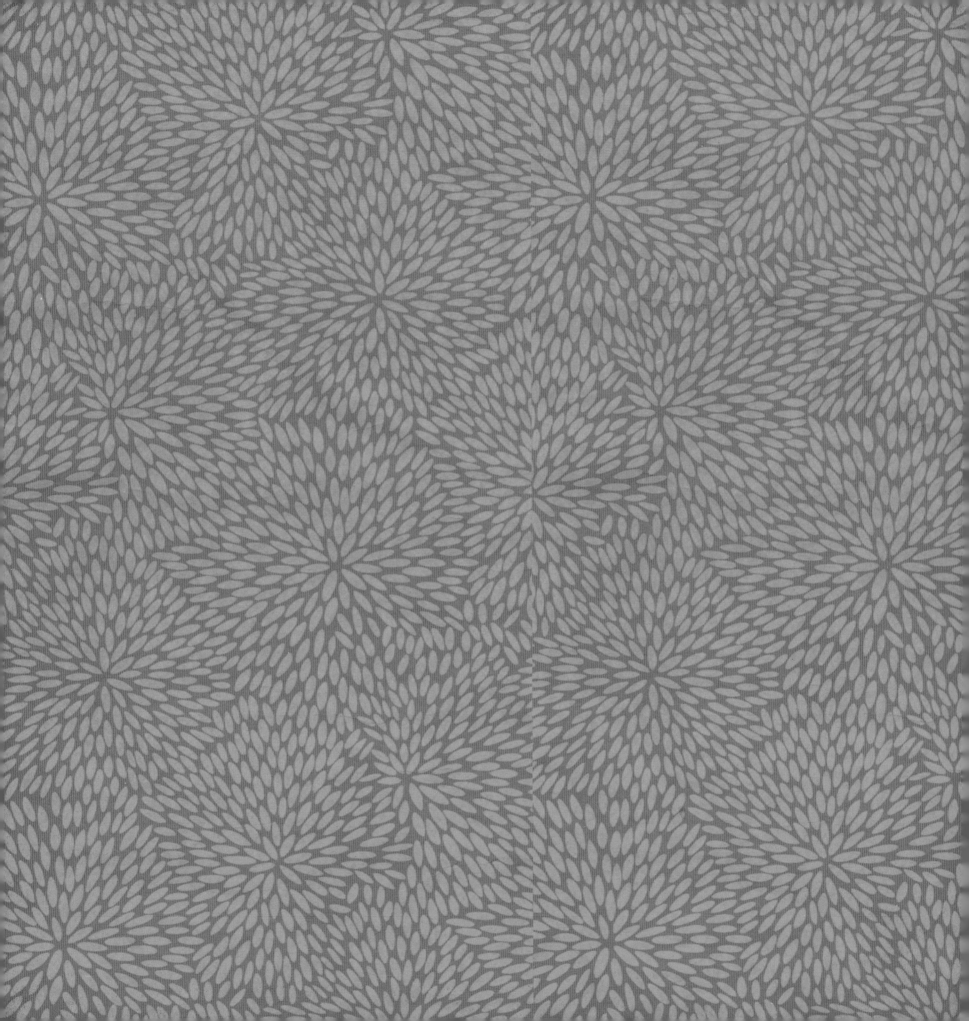